WITHDRAWN

P9-AZW-364

EF-RYL   Rylant, Cynthia.
                The high-rise
        private eyes

                        1st ed.

WR   '03

MOUNT LAUREL LIBRARY

100 Walt Whitman Avenue

Mount Laurel, NJ 08054

856-234-7319

www.mtlaurel.lib.nj.us

DEMCO

In a high-rise building
deep in the heart of a big city
live two private eyes:
Bunny Brown and Jack Jones.
Bunny is the brains,
Jack is the snoop,
and together they
crack cases wide open.

This is the story of
Case Number 005:
THE CASE OF
THE SLEEPY SLOTH.

story by
Cynthia Rylant

pictures by
G. Brian Karas

THE
HIGH-RISE
PRIVATE
EYES

Out to
Lunch

Mount Laurel Library
100 Walt Whitman Avenue
Mt. Laurel, NJ 08054-9539
(856) 234-7319

The High-Rise Private Eyes

The Case of
the Sleepy
Sloth

Greenwillow Books
An Imprint of HarperCollinsPublishers

For Virginia
—C. R.

To Mrs. Dedrick and her eager readers
—G. B. K.

The High-Rise Private Eyes: The Case of the Sleepy Sloth
Text copyright © 2002 by Cynthia Rylant
Illustrations copyright © 2002 by G. Brian Karas
All rights reserved.
Printed in Hong Kong
by South China Printing Company (1988) Ltd.
www.harperchildrens.com

Acrylic, gouache, and pencil were used for the full-color art.
The text type is Times.

Library of Congress Cataloging-in-Publication Data
Rylant, Cynthia
The high-rise private eyes: the case of the sleepy sloth /
by Cynthia Rylant ; pictures by G. Brian Karas.
  p. cm.
"Greenwillow Books."
Summary: While having a picnic on the docks, animal
detectives Bunny and Jack meet a dog whose one and only
lawn chair is missing, and they set out to solve the case.
ISBN 0-06-009098-7 (trade). ISBN 0-06-009099-5 (lib. bdg.)
[1. Animals—Fiction. 2. Mystery and detective stories.]
I. Title: Case of the sleepy sloth. II. Karas, G. Brian, ill. III. Title.
PZ7.R982 Hqe 2002 [E]—dc21 2001054729

1 2 3 4 5 6 7 8 9 10 First Edition

Contents

Chapter 1
Pizza

Bunny and Jack
liked to picnic with pizza.
Jack brought the pizza,
Bunny brought the pop,
and they went to the docks downtown.

"Now, don't give the seagulls
any pizza," said Bunny.
"They'll just linger."
"But they always look
so hungry," said Jack.

"That's because they *are*

always hungry," said Bunny.

"If you gave a seagull

twenty-five pizzas,

he'd still be hungry.

Seagulls eat.

That's their job."

"Cool job," said Jack.

"Just remember," said Bunny.

"Don't share."

"Don't share," said Jack.

"Do not share," Bunny said.

"Do not share," Jack said again.

"Want a slice of pizza?"

Jack asked a seagull walking by.

"Sure!" said the seagull.

"I don't believe it," said Bunny.

Soon several more seagulls

showed up.

They lingered and lingered.

Jack passed out slices of pizza

while Bunny said,

"I don't believe it"

over and over.

Soon all the pizza was gone.

Then the seagulls were gone.

"What did I do?" asked Jack.

"You gave away all our pizza,"
  said Bunny.

"I did?" asked Jack.

"You did," said Bunny.

"I don't believe it," said Jack.

"Ditto," said Bunny.

"Stop me next time," said Jack.

"Next time we'll eat pizza inside,"
  said Bunny.

"With no lingering seagulls,"
  said Jack.

"Right," said Bunny.

"But no cool boats either,"
  said Jack.

Bunny looked around.

"That's true," she said.

"Or blue sky," said Jack.

"That's true," said Bunny.

"Or sunshine," said Jack.

"That's true," said Bunny.

"Or weird dogs
   in yellow pants," said Jack.

"That's . . . What?" asked Bunny.

"That dog over there
    is snooping around that boat,"
    said Jack. "Pretty weird."
"Hmmmm," said Bunny.
    They watched as the dog
    snooped around the sailboat,
    then snooped under a dock.
"That is a sneaky, snoopy puppy,"
    said Jack.
"Yes," said Bunny.
"Bet you can't say it ten times,"
    said Jack.

"Say what?" asked Bunny.

"'Sneaky snoopy puppy,'" said Jack.

"Oh, for heaven's sake," said Bunny.

"Just try," said Jack.

"No," said Bunny.

"Okay, three times," said Jack.

"No," said Bunny.

"Okay, once," said Jack.

"If I say it once,
   will you go over
   and ask that dog what he's doing?"
   asked Bunny.
"Twice," said Jack.
"Oh, all right," said Bunny.
"Sneaky snoopy puppy,
   sneaky smoopy puppy."

"You said 'smoopy,'" said Jack.

"Did not," said Bunny.

"Did," said Jack.

"Did not," said Bunny.

"Did," said Jack.

"And now I'm going over
to see what that smoopy puppy
is up to."

"Ugh," said Bunny.

Chapter 2
The Case

"Hi. I'm Jack,"

said Jack to the dog.

The dog shook Jack's hand.

"I'm Ramón," he said.

"Lose something?" asked Jack.

"Yes, indeed," said Ramón.

"My one and only lawn chair."

"Your one and only lawn chair?"

asked Jack.

"Yes," said Ramón.

"It disappeared on Monday."

"Disappeared?" asked Jack. "Cool!

Hey, Bunny!" he called.

"We have a case!"

"Did you say 'cool?'"
asked Ramón.

"Oh, sorry," said Jack.

"I just get all tingly
when things disappear."

"What's the problem?"
asked Bunny, walking up.

"This smoopy . . .

　I mean, this nice dog here

　has lost his lawn chair," said Jack.

"His one and only."

　Ramón looked at Bunny.

"Have you seen my chair?"

　he asked her.

"No," said Bunny,

"but I can probably find it."

"We," said Jack.

"*We* can probably find it."

"*We* are private eyes," said Bunny.

She took out her notepad.

"May I ask you a few questions?"

"Okay," said Ramón.

"When did you last see the chair?"

asked Bunny.

"Monday," said Ramón and Jack.

Everyone looked at Jack.

"Oops, sorry," said Jack.

"I love knowing the answer."

"And *where* did you last see
the chair?" asked Bunny, writing.

"On the deck of my houseboat,"
said Ramón.

"You live on a houseboat?"
asked Jack. "Cool!"

"What kind of lawn chair?" asked Bunny.

"Redwood, iron, cheap fold-up . . . ?"

"Cheap fold-up," said Ramón.

"We should search the houseboat,"
  said Jack.

"Why?" asked Bunny.

"The chair's not there."

"Yes, but houseboats are cool,"
  said Jack.

"So where do *you* live?" asked Ramón.

"In that high-rise over there,"
  said Jack.

"Cool," said Ramón, looking up.

"I'm on the ground floor," said Jack.

"Oh. Not cool," said Ramón.

"I fear heights," said Jack.

"Really?" said Ramón.

"I fear earthquakes."

"But we don't get earthquakes here,"
  said Jack.

"Exactly," said Ramón.

"GUYS!" said Bunny.

"Can we please solve this case?"

Suddenly a big gust of wind

blew the notepad

out of Bunny's hands.

"Hey!" said Bunny.

Then a ball, a box,

and a pink flamingo blew by.

"Somebody's really going to miss

that flamingo," said Jack.

Then Jack looked at Bunny.

Bunny looked at Jack.

And they both said, *"Bingo!"*

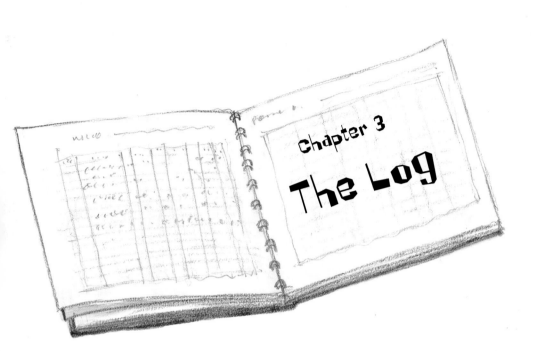

Chapter 3

The Log

Jack and Bunny
went with Ramón
to his houseboat.
His boating log
would tell them
which way the wind blew
on Monday.

"I told you we needed
to see the houseboat,"
Jack said to Bunny.
"You just wanted to play,"
said Bunny.
"Who doesn't?" said Jack.

"Well," said Bunny,

"when we find out

    which way the lawn chair blew,

    it won't take long

    to close this case."

"Oh, good," said Ramón.

"I miss my chair."

"It's his one and only,"

    Jack said to Bunny.

"I heard," Bunny said.

Jack loved Ramón's houseboat.

"Hey," said Jack. "Cozy."

"And no earthquakes," said Ramón.

"Right," said Jack.

"The log says the wind
    was blowing south on Monday,"
    said Bunny. "Let's go."

"Hey, I wanted to pretend-steer,"
  said Jack, standing at the wheel.
"Next time," said Bunny.
"Should I come along?"
  asked Ramón.
"No need," said Bunny.
"We should be back pronto
  with your lawn chair."

"We might be hungry," said Jack.

"Come on, Jack," said Bunny.

"We might need a snack," said Jack.

"Come on," said Bunny,

   pulling him out the door.

"Like COOKIES!"

   Jack called behind him.

"CHOCOLATE CHIP!

   SORT OF MELTY!"

Chapter 4
Solved

Bunny and Jack

went from boat to boat to boat.

No lawn chair.

Then, near the end of the dock,

they saw it.

Somebody was sitting in it.

"Here goes," said Bunny.

"Excuse me!" she called.
Bunny and Jack walked over
to the person in the lawn chair.
It was an old sloth, sleeping.
"Hello?" said Bunny.

"AH-HEM!" said Jack loudly.

The old sloth slept.

"Can I help you?"

said a voice behind them.

"Whoa," said Jack with a jump.

"Sorry. I didn't mean to startle you."

The voice belonged

to a younger sloth.

"That's my auntie," she said.

Bunny and Jack introduced themselves.

They explained about the lawn chair.

"Oh, dear," said the young sloth,

whose name was Ruth.

"When the chair blew in,

Auntie sat down

and went right to sleep."

"Auntie's been asleep
  since *Monday*?" said Jack.

"Sloths sleep a lot," said Ruth.

"I'll say," said Jack.

"When do you think
  she'll wake up?" asked Bunny.

"Maybe next Friday?" said Ruth.

"You're kidding," said Jack.

"Will you take the chair
  back to Ramón's houseboat then?"
  asked Bunny.

"I promise," said Ruth.

Bunny and Jack

walked back to the houseboat.

"Wow, some nap," said Jack.

"I'll say," said Bunny.

"And how about that name?" said Jack.

"What name?" asked Bunny.

"Ruth," said Jack. "Ruth Sloth.

It makes your tongue funny."

"I hadn't noticed," said Bunny.

"Say it," said Jack.

"Say what?" asked Bunny.

"Ruth Sloth," said Jack.

"Say it ten times."

"No," said Bunny.

"How about 'Smoopy Ruth Sloth?'"
    said Jack.

"Can you say that?"

"No, but I can say,

'*Can it,*'" said Bunny.

"Oh, you can, can you?" said Jack.

"Hmmmm," said Bunny.

"Do you smell what I smell?"
    Jack smelled.

"Chocolate chip cookies!" he said.

"Hurray, Ramón!"

"Don't forget, Jack," said Bunny.

"Don't feed the seagulls."

"No way," said Jack.

"Promise?" asked Bunny.

"Promise," said Jack.

"Do not share," said Bunny.

"Do not share," said Jack.

A seagull walked by.

"Maybe we should eat inside,"

said Jack.

"Ditto," said Bunny with a smile.

Mount Laurel Library
100 Walt Whitman Avenue
Mt. Laurel, NJ 08054-9539
(856) 234-7319

Feed
Me!